SOMEONE IS TALKING ABOUT HORTENSE

STORY BY LAURETTE MURDOCK
PICTURES BY JAMES MARSHALL

HOUGHTON MIFFLIN COMPANY BOSTON

www.hmco.com/trade

Library of Congress Catalog Card Number: 00132438
ISBN 0-618-07318-3

Manufactured in the Singapore
TWP 10 9 8 7 6 5 4 3 2 1

FOR
MY DAUGHTERS
MARY AND
SARA
L.M.

Hortense didn't know what made her wake up. She couldn't hear or see anything, but she had a feeling that someone was talking about her. It made her uneasy. Was it something in the air?

She tiptoed to the bathroom and looked out the window, but there was nobody there. She ran warm water in the tub and stepped in daintily. “Someone is talking about me!” she said in her squeakiest voice.

IT is
FUN
TO BE
CLEAN

Hortense could hardly get on with her housework. At noon there was an awful smell of burning. She ran to the kitchen and looked in the oven. There in the roasting pan was a black shriveled lump. "Imagine forgetting my Sunday roast! That just shows how upset I am."

HOME
SWEET
HOME

She threw the butter in the trash can and shut the dustpan in the refrigerator. Again she was sure she heard someone saying her name, but there was no one around.

"Maybe if I go for a stroll in the park this silly feeling will go away," thought Hortense. She put on her shawl and hurried down the street. All the way she heard a buzzing in the trees.

But around the corner there was only Owl perched on a railing.

"Owl," said Hortense, "was that you talking about me?" Owl stretched his wings and said, "Who me?"

"Do you ever hear voices when there is no one there?" asked Hortense.

"No," said Owl, "and if I did I wouldn't take any notice."

In the park Hortense saw two of her best friends. They were talking about something.

"Let's change the subject," said Miss Bulldog when Hortense drew close.

"Good afternoon, Hortense," they said. "It's too bad we were just leaving."

“What an odd way for best friends to behave,” thought Hortense.

At the water fountain, Hortense saw her friend Miss Duck making a telephone call.

When Miss Duck saw Hortense, she hung up the receiver with a bang and waddled off in the opposite direction.

“O my goodness,” thought Hortense.

TELEPHONE
FOUNTAIN

Right away Hortense went to see her friend Mrs. Parrot, who was known to be very sensible, and asked if she ever had the feeling that someone was talking about her. Mrs. Parrot said, "Sit down in this rocker and I'll make tea. Now, my dear," she said soothingly, "are you sure this isn't just your imagination? You'll feel better if you take a nice long walk."

This advice didn't make Hortense feel any better, but she said "thanks."

Hortense knew that an ice cream soda would make her feel better. She was enjoying the first creamy sip when she heard voices in the next booth. "Do you think Hortense knows?...Come on, we must hurry."

CHILI DOGS
NO SLURPING!
OUR SUNDAES ARE YUMMY!
TRY OUR ICKY FUDGE

On the way home again Hortense sat down on a bench and thought some more about what she had just heard. She just couldn't understand it.

At her front door Hortense could hear talking and laughing. In *her* house!

Then the door flew open and there were all her friends! On the table was a huge cake with lovely icing and beautiful rosettes.

"Happy Birthday!" they all sang. "You were right, Hortense, everyone *was* talking about you!"

THE END

Laurette Murdock, a writer, painter, gardener, and restorer of old houses, thought the next best thing to having a raccoon for a pet was to write a story about one. Ms. Murdock traveled extensively in Greece, France, Italy, and Hong Kong, and worked as a copy editor for a major publishing company.

James Marshall, the creator of many hilarious books for children, including *Miss Nelson Is Missing* and *The Stupids Step Out,* has no rival when it comes to goofy fun. Filled with the same silly spirit and charm, his *Four Little Troubles* provide cozy comfort to young readers facing the universal troubles of childhood.

The *Four Little Troubles* series includes:
Eugene
Sing Out, Irene
Snake: His Story
Someone Is Talking about Hortense, written by Laurette Murdock